Anonymous

England in Rhyme

Or History for the Young of the Kings and Queens in England

Anonymous

England in Rhyme
Or History for the Young of the Kings and Queens in England

ISBN/EAN: 9783337271831

Printed in Europe, USA, Canada, Australia, Japan

Cover: Foto ©Andreas Hilbeck / pixelio.de

More available books at **www.hansebooks.com**

ENGLAND IN RHYME:

OR,

History for the Young

OF THE

Kings and Queens of England.

NEW YORK:

Carleton, Publisher, 413 *Broadway.*

(LATE RUDD & CARLETON.)

M DCCC LXII.

R. CRAIGHEAD,
Printer, Stereotyper, and Electrotyper,
Carton Building,
81, 83, and 85 Centre Street.

PREFACE.

THE earliest, and at the same time the most attractive lessons taught in the nursery, are bits of biography. As instances we need only mention The Queen of Hearts, Tom the Piper's Son, Mother Hubbard, Jenny Wren, and Dr. Forster—immortal personages, whose names and deeds are imbedded deep in the strata of memory. With no vain wish to supersede these worthies, the author, taking a hint from their fame, has endeavored to implant in the mind the germs of real history; and hence the attempt has been made to connect the names of the Sovereigns of England with some leading historical fact or trait of personal character. These unpolished rhymes have at least one advantage over the most charming fiction. When an inquisitive child pointedly asks its mother if the story is true, she can without hesitation answer—Yes.

I.

William I.

Born 1023.]   [*Began to reign* 1066.

WILLIAM the I., as the Conqueror known,
By the battle of Hastings ascended the throne.
His acts were all made in the Norman tongue,
And at eight every evening the curfew was rung,
When each English subject, by royal desire,
Extinguished his candle and put out his fire.
He bridled the kingdom with forts round the border,
And the Tower of London was built by his order.

Died 1087.

II.

William II.

Born 1056.]   [*Began to reign* 1087.

WILLIAM styled Rufus, from having red hair,
Of virtue possessed but a moderate share.
But though he was one whom we covetous call,
He built the famed structure, Westminster Hall.
Walter Tyrrel, his favorite, whilst hunting one day,
Attempted a deer with an arrow to slay,
But missing his aim, struck the King to the heart.
His body was carried away in a cart.

Died 1100.

III.

Henry I.

Born 1068.]   [*Began to reign* 1108.

KING HENRY the First, for his learning much famed,
Beauclerc or fine scholar, was justly surnamed:
His subjects revered him, and not without cause—
He lightened their burdens, restored their old laws,
Abolished the curfew, bad money put down,
And kindly remitted the dues of the crown.
But Henry was frail, and licentious beside,
And at last, by a surfeit of lampreys he died.

Died 1135.

IV.

Stephen.

Born 1085.]   [*Began to reign* 1135.

Kɪɴɢ Henry's demise was no sooner made known
Than Stephen contrived to step up to the throne.
By arts and by wiles, he the clergy secured,
And by popular actions the people allured.
And though for a time, through his rival's success,
He felt, as a captive, the deepest distress,
His fortune once more placed the crown on his brow,
And there it continued, till death laid him low.

Died 1154.

V.

Henry II.

Born 1132.]   [*Began to reign* 1154.

KING HENRY the II., Plantagenet called,
In disputes and vexations was sadly enthralled,
His consort was jealous, his sons took up arms,
Proud Becket, too, filled him with serious alarms ;
And when that archbishop had met with his doom,
The monarch was scourged by the side of the tomb ;
Then paving the streets made London look pretty,
And houses no longer were thatched in the city.

Died 1189.

VI.

Richard I.

Born 1157.]   [*Began to reign* 1189.

KING RICHARD the I. next ascended the throne,
Whose valour, no doubt, to the reader is known,
With the heart of a lion all danger he faced,
And the famous Crusades with his presence he graced,
But forced by a storm upon Italy's coast
This lover of fighting his liberty lost.
Thrice five tedious months in confinement he stayed,
And then a vast sum for his ransom was paid.

Died 1199.

VII.

John.

Born 1167.] [*Began to reign* 1199

John, surnamed Lackland, 'tis said to his shame,
To the Pontiff of Rome a mean vassal became,
His barons, indignant, then marshalled their bands,
And famed *Magna Charta* obtained from his hands,
But charters and oaths were unable to bind
A monarch possessing so treacherous a mind.
His standard he raised, and his influence tried,
But fever assailed him, he sickened and died.

Died 1216.

VIII.

Henry III.

Born 1207.]   [*Began to reign* 1216.

THEN next in succession was Henry the Third,
Who seldom regarded his oath or his word,
The sums he exacted he lavishly spent,
And showed his profusion wherever he went.
His barons at length were in battle arrayed,
And Henry, at Lewes, a prisoner was made.
But peace was restored after Leicester was slain,
And war waxed no more till the end of the reign.

Died 1272.

IX.

Edward I.

Born 1239.]   [*Began to reign* 1272.

The first Edward, called Longchamp, from all that
Was very successful, but very severe.   [we hear,
In Wales and in Scotland his barons he spread,
And the blood of their poets and warriors he shed.
In London alone, of the Jews, as they say,
Two hundred and eighty he hanged in one day;
But this as an act of stern justice was done,
And a Prince the Welsh found in the birth of his son.

Died 1307

X.

Edward II.

Born 1284.]   [*Began to reign* 1307.

King Edward the II., Caernarvon surnamed,
Was chiefly for follies and suffering famed,
His favorites his time and affections engrossed,
Till his queen proved untrue, and his sceptre was lost.
Depossed and despised, to the Tower he went,
And from prison to prison was afterwards sent,
There at leisure he mourned over scenes that were past,
And by ruffians was cruelly murdered at last.

Died 1327.

XI.

Edward III.

Born 1312.]   [*Began to reign* 1327.

For Edward the III., as historians relate,
The love and respect of his subjects were great.
In France and in Scotland most bravely he fought,
And their monarchs to England he prisoners brought.
He built Windsor Castle, and writers have stated,
The Knights of the Garter by him were created;
To science and merit his name was endeared,
And now the reformer, John Wickliffe, appeared.

Died 1377.

XII.

Richard II.

Born 1367.]   [*Began to reign* 1377.

KING Richard the II., as we have been told,
Ascended the throne when eleven years old,
Wat Tyler's rebellion he soon overthrew,
Yet proved himself weak and impolitic too;
His barons took arms and resisted his power,
And forced him to seek a retreat in the Tower.
His crown he resigned, but resigned it in vain,
For in Pontefract Castle poor Richard was slain.

Died 1100.

XIII.

Richard II.

Born 1367.]   [*Began to reign* 1399.

Whenn Richard the II. to prison was driven,
To Lancaster's Duke the dominion was given;
But scarcely had Henry been solemnly crowned,
When plots and rebellions began to abound;
But by vigour and promptitude these were suppressed,
And many abuses were partly redressed.
In this reign the first blood of the Lollards was spilt,
Famed Whittingham lived and Guildhall was rebuilt.

Died 1413.

XIV.

Henry V.

Born 1388.]   [*Began to reign* 1413.

Famed Henry the V. next ascended the throne,
And soon to the French was his bravery known,
Though sick and fatigued, and in numbers but few,
His troops were enabled the foe to subdue,
On Agincourt's field, which will long live in story,
For there British soldiers were covered with glory.
Fresh conquests succeeded, but Henry's career
Was cut short by grim death in his thirty-fourth year.

Died 1422.

XV.

Henry VI.

Born 1421.]   [*Began to reign* 1422.

Of splendour unconscious, to govern unable,
King Henry the VI. was a babe in his cradle;
In London and Paris they crowned this poor child,
Who, when he grew up, proved weak, merciful, mild;
But weak were his measures and feeble his sway,
France was lost, and the English refused to obey;
Civil war soon blazed out, plots on plots were disclosed,
York triumphed in arms and the king was deposed.

Died 1461.

XVI.

Edward IV.

Born 1443.]   [*Began to reign* 1461.

In Edward the IV. a stern king we behold,
Of whom many terrible tales have been told;
In the field he was brave, but tyrannic at best,
And cruelty held its dire reign in his breast.
His legalized murders in history look black,
His brother he drowned in a butt of sweet sack;
For an innocent jest he would chop off a head,
And terror prevailed till the tyrant was dead.

Died 1483.

XVII.

Edward V.

Born 1470.]   [*Began to reign* 1483.

Young Edward the V. was a king but in name,

His uncle, regardless of sin and of shame,

Both him and his brother deprived of their sight,

And caused the poor boys to be smothered at night.

In a chest at the foot of the staircase they lay,

Till a hundred and ninety-one years rolled away,

Then to Westminster Abbey their dust was removed,

As the lines on their monument clearly have proved.

Died 1483.

XVIII.

Richard III.

Born 1450.]   [*Began to reign* 1483.

The monarch called Crookback, or Richard the III.,
Of whom many tragical stories you've heard,
Was sullen, reserved, cruel, treacherous, and base,
To England a scourge, and a stain to his race;
Detested he lived, and detested he died,
For though brave, he possessed not a virtue beside.
At Richmond, near Bosworth, the tyrant was slain,
In his thirty-fourth year and the third of his reign.

Died 1485.

XIX.

Henry VII.

Born 1457.]   [*Began to reign* 1485.

In Henry the VII. and his consort we find
The houses of York and Lancaster combined,
And though two pretenders laid claim to the crown,
Both Simnel and Warbeck were shortly put down.
Though Henry loved money, he reared to his fame
The beautiful chapel which still bears his name.
In his reign the West Indies were likewise found out,
And at Richmond, in Surrey, he died of the gout.

Died 1509.

XX.

Henry VIII.

Born 1492.]   [*Began to reign* 1509.

Now comes the Eighth Henry in royal array,
The Blue-Beard of England, historians say;
Who by passion incited, or jealousy led,
Thought nothing of shortening his wives by a head.
Divorces and murders astonished the nation,
The monks lost their cash in the new reformation;
Great Cardinal Wolsey was left in the lurch, [church.
And the King lived and died supreme head of the

Died 1547.

XXI.

Edward VI.

Born 1537.]　　　　　　　　[*Began to reign* 1547.

KING Edward the VI., when but nine years of age,
Ascended the throne with the mind of a sage;
The Latin and French he could fluently speak,
And understood Spanish, Italian, and Greek;　[ed,
He founded Christ's Hospital, crowns were first coin-
And half crowns beside, as in history we find,
He favoured the cause of the great reformation,
But died at sixteen, to the grief of the nation.

Died 1553.

XXII.

Mary.

Born 1516.]   [Began to reign 1553.

In Mary, the consort of Philip, was seen
A furious bigot, a merciless queen.
The Duke of Northumberland, Lady Jane Gray
And her lord, to the scaffold were all led away;
And Ridley, and Cranmer, and Latimer died
As martyrs, with hundreds of subjects beside;
But Heaven interposed bleeding England to save,
And Mary, detested, sank into her grave.

Died 1558.

XXIII.

𝕰𝖑𝖎𝖟𝖆𝖇𝖊𝖙𝖍.

Born 1533.]   [*Began to reign* 1558.

ELIZABETH next had a glorious reign,
She aided the Protestants, humbled proud Spain;
The boasted Armada her warriors o'erthrew,
And its spoils in the Tower our readers may view.
But Scotia's unfortunate queen claims a sigh,
And Essex, the favorite, was sentenced to die.
The Royal Exchange was now built, it is said,
And gunpowder, first, by the English was made.

Died 1603.

XXIV.

James I.

Born 1556.]   [*Began to reign* 1603.

James the I., who in learning and hunting delighted,
The crowns of old England and Scotland united;
And though in the air he was doomed to be blown,
He found out the plot, and remained on the throne.
In this reign a translation of Scriptures was made,
His foes the great Raleigh to ruin betrayed.
The New River to town from Hertford was brought,
And whales on the coast of Greenland were caught.

Died 1625.

XXV.

Charles I.

Born 1600.]   [*Began to reign* 1625.

Charles the I. to prerogative strongly inclined,
Involved in a civil commotion we find.
He fought and he struggled, but all proved in vain,
His son was made prisoner, his forces were slain.
The Parliament triumphed, the King was deposed,
And a scaffold the scene of his sufferings closed.
Though Littleton says, who his history penned,
He excelled as a husband, a father, a friend.

Beheaded 1649.

XXVI.

Oliver Cromwell.

Born 1599.]   [*Made Protector* 1653.

Insidious and crafty, though brave without doubt,
Was Cromwell, who turned the Long Parliament out,
Who the government into a commonwealth framed,
And Protector of England was solemnly named.
But though his ambition was crowned with success,
His life was embittered by anxious distress.
And when he expired such a hurricane blew,
As never was witnessed by me or by you.

Died 1658.

XXVII.

Charles II.

Born 1630.]   [*Began to reign* 1660.

WHILE Cromwell was styled Protector at home,
Charles the II. was doomed as an exile to roam.
But when Oliver died, by consent of the nation,
General Monk soon effected the King's restoration.
In this reign the Great Fire of London occurred,
And Blood stole the crown from the Tower I've heard.
The Thames was so frozen that coaches plied there,
And booths were erected, resembling a fair.

Died 1685.

XXVIII.

James II.

Born 1633.]   [*Began to reign* 1685.

James the II. had scarcely ascended the throne,
When his folly and bigotry both were made known,
The Protestant faith he resolved to o'erthrow,
And did by degrees, all a tyrant can do.
The brave Duke of Monmouth attempted in vain,
The nation to rouse, and their rights to regain;
But William of Orange more fortunate proved,
And the bigoted Prince from the kingdom removed.

Abdicated 1688.

XXIX.

William III.

Born 1650.]   [*Began to reign* 1689.

GREAT William, judicious, sagacious, and brave,
Came forward Great Britain to succor and save;
And Britons by feelings of gratitude led,
Placed the crown on the great deliverer's head.
With Mary his consort he happily reigned,
And in battle fresh laurels he constantly gained.
The famed Bank of England now first claimed atten-
And historians now the first bayonets mention. [tion,

Died 1702.

XXX.

Queen Anne.

Born 1664.]   [Began to reign 1702.

GREAT Anne, who commanders of merit employed,
A series of glorious successes enjoyed,
And spite of all fears and all factions beside,
Truly honored she lived, and lamented she died.
In this reign the fine mansion of Blenheim was raised
For Marlborough's Duke, so deservedly praised.
And now flourished Swift, Arbuthnot, and Rowe,
With Bolingbroke, Pope, and more than you know.

Died 1714.

XXXI.

George I.

Born 1660.]   [*Began to reign* 1714.

George the I., as Elector of Hanover known,
Succeeded illustrious Anne on the throne ;
And acted so prudently in his new station,
As to gain the respect and esteem of the nation.
Now Parliament men were for seven years elected,
The South Sea delusion was formed and detected.
To prevent small-pox a new method was tried,
And the King on a journey at Osnaburgh died.

Died 1727.

XXXII.

George II.

Born 1683.]   [Began to reign 1727.

G EORGE the II., though plain in his mode of address,
Swayed the sceptre of Britain with brilliant success;
His virtues more useful than splendid appeared,
But his justice was spotless, his name was revered.
Rebellion was crushed, and good order maintained,
Whilst by sea and by land many victories he gained.
The British Museum now opened to view,   [new.
And the Old Style was changed, in this reign, for the

Died 1760.

XXXIII.

George III.

Born 1738.]   [*Began to reign* 1760.

George the III. of his people the father and friend,
Acted well through his reign from beginning to end.
When the French revolution astonished the world,
And kings from their thrones were rapidly hurled,
Unappalled by the storm, every danger he braved,
And by firmness his kingdom from anarchy saved.
His reign was extended, let Heaven have the praise,
To fifty-nine years, three months, and four days.

Died 1820.

XXXIV.

George IV.

Born 1762.]   [*Began to reign* 1820.

GEORGE the IV., when his patriot father was gone,
By right of succession ascended the throne ;
To Hanover, Ireland, and Scotland he went,
Where his time and his money he cheerfully spent ;
Famed Windsor's old castle, this monarch repaired,
And near Buckingham Gate a new palace he reared.

Died 1830.

XXXV.

William IV.

Born 1765.]   [*Began to reign* 1830.

THEN William the IV. took his seat on the throne,
With his excellent queen, for he ruled not alone;
When round him arose the political storm,
He braved the rude billows and granted reform.
His reign was but short, but the heart in his breast,
Gathered round him the bravest, and wisest, and best.
And on Britain's broad banner his name is unfurled,
As a King of old England, and friend of the world.

Died 1837.

XXXVI.

Victoria.

Born 1819.]   [*Began to reign* 1837.

THE Princess Victoria, when only eighteen,
Took her seat on the throne of old England as Queen.
Ye Britons! with virtue and valour attend,
Be prompt to uphold her and strong to defend.
May justice and mercy, and goodness and truth,
Like a sunbeam adorn the bright brow of her youth.
May oppression beneath her mild sceptre bow down,
And her heart find delight in her country's renown.

The End.